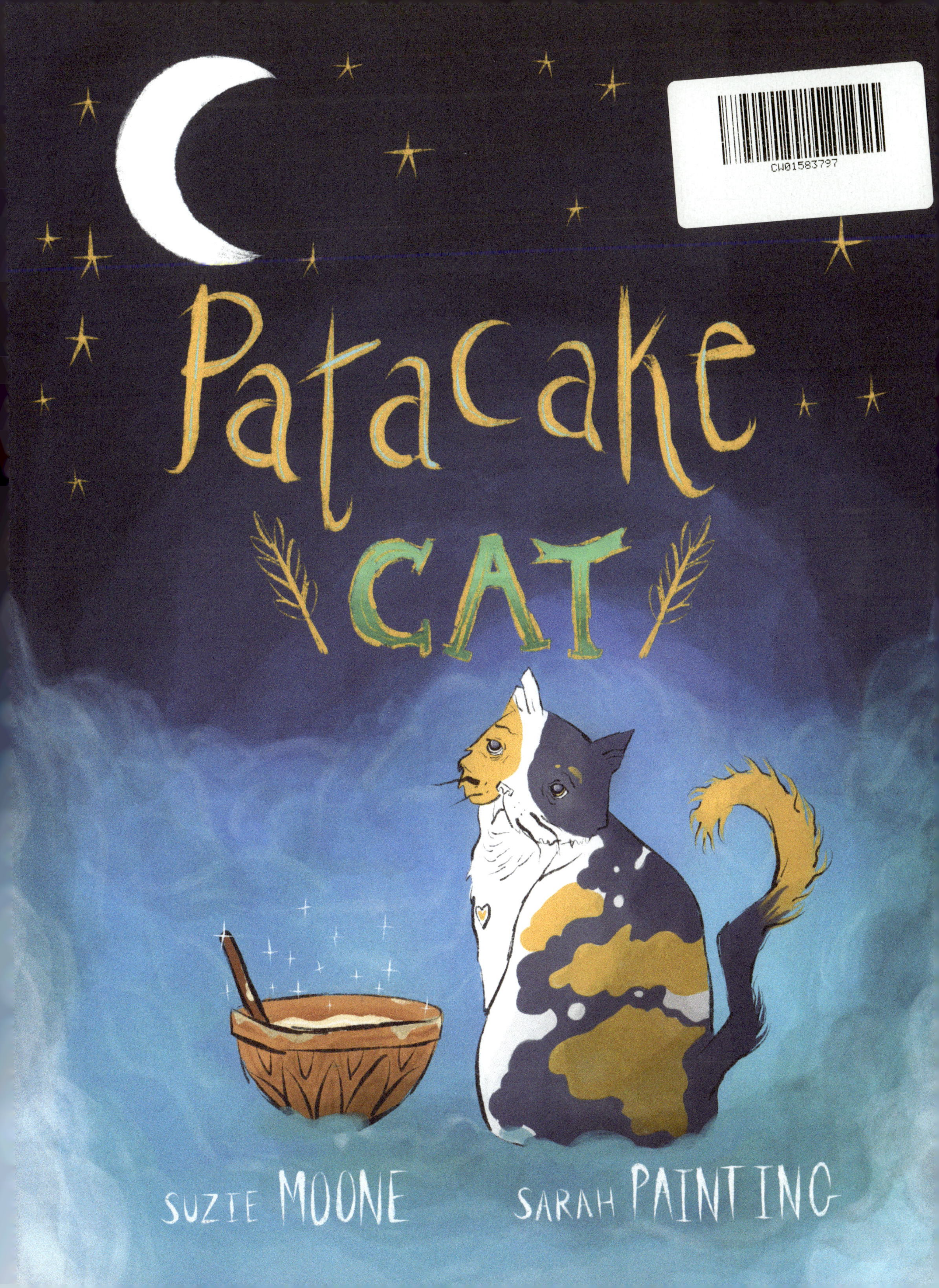
Patacake
CAT
SUZIE MOONE
SARAH PAINTING

ISBN: 9781999968885

Edited by E. Rachael Hardcastle
Formatted by E. Rachael Hardcastle
Written by Suzie Moone
Illustrated by Sarah Painting

Published by Curious Cat Books, United Kingdom
For further information: www.curiouscatbooks.co.uk

1st Edition

Patacake Cat was as blind as a bat,
With raggedy calico fur,
His question mark tail raised as high as a sail,
Like the pitch of his cheerful purr.

Patacake Cat owned a fellow named Gus,
And a baker was Gus by his trade,
The cat spent his days in the flour dust haze,
Of the bakery where his bed was made.

Patacake Cat dozed for most of the day,
By the warmth of the oven he lazed,
While Gus laboured long ‘til his arms were not strong,
And his eyes were all tired and glazed.

Patacake Cat watched the orders stack up,
And townsfolk leave vexed and unfed,
“I cannot keep track, my best efforts still lack,
Oh, what will I do?” Gus said.

Patacake Cat would knead his bed,
To make it so cosy and warm,
While Gus watched his cat kneading this way and that,
An idea began to form.

"Patacake Cat, you can earn your keep,
Under the indigo sky,
By the pearly white moon you can make us doubloon,
In cakes, loaves, pudding and pie.

You take the night shift and I'll take the day,
Together we'll get the job done,
My workload be spliced for a comfortable life,
For both of us rather than one."

Patacake Cat was not certain that,
His comfort he wanted to trade,
For hard working shifts in the flour dust sift,
Of the bakery where his bed was laid.

He looked at the face of the man he owned,
Worry stitched all through his brow,
And at last he agreed so they may succeed,
Gus really did need *him* now.

Patacake Cat was apprenticed to bake,
By the light of the silvery moon,
Beneath Gus's watchful eyes, he made bread, loaves and pies,
And cookies to tell your fortune.

News spread afar of the calico cat,
Who baked in the eventide calm,
The villagers left satisfied, not bereft,
As pennies for bread loaves crossed palm.

Patacake Cat stayed up all the nights long,
'Til the evening stars hid for the morn,
He watched the sun rise like his cakes, loaves and pies,
As dewdrops bejewelled the dawn.

Patacake Cat had honed his craft,
To knead and to roll and to bake,
News of his skills spread far over the hills,
Until the queen then requested a cake!

Patacake Cat made the finest cake,
The baker ever did see,
Bespangled with stars and dust gathered from Mars,
And moon glow composed of the sea.

He delivered it prompt to the palace on foot,
In the eerie green light of the dawn,
Alas the proud queen found it far from pristine,
The adornments were vanished by morn.

She said, "I will grant you but one final chance,
Yourself and your skills to redeem,
We all have off days, now try to amaze,
Make one which befits my esteem."

So Patacake nervously took up his tools,
And started to try once more,
The world's finest cake he proceeded to make,
This had to impress, he was sure!

The cake was festooned with borrowed moonlight,
And garlanded hundreds of stars,
It was iced with the shine of the roiling sea brine,
And copper dust gathered from Mars.

When it was finished, Patacake trudged,
Up the dark, lonely path to the palace,
With the cake in a sack on his weary back,
To strive to please haughty Queen Alice.

Approaching, he said to the guard at the gates,
"Please dispatch this cake before dawn,
There's no time to waste; don't tarry, make haste,
Or the decor be ruined by morn."

The sentry did run to her chambers at once,
To deliver the cake whilst she slept,
He dared to awaken the Queen, she was shaken,
"What's so important?" she wept.

He opened the sack and looked at the cake,
His jaw dropped with worry and wonder,
"My Queen, pardon me, this you really must see,
Pirates preparing to plunder!"

He showed her the cake and she too was aghast,
She could scarcely believe her own eyes,
For the cake's borrowed moon and its starlight bestrewn,
Showed a scene from the bay of Belsize.

The waves on the cake rolled, frothed and churned,
And by the light of the silvery moon,
Marauders embroiled, dishonestly toiled,
On a ship docked within the lagoon.

“The cake is an omen!” she shouted in shock,
“We must protect our fair village!
From the villainous knaves of the night and the waves,
In the bay getting ready to pillage.”

The queen sent her men by two score and ten,
To the bay on horseback and on foot,
Where indeed it was found a ship was aground,
With pirates preparing to loot.

The queen being clever had ordered her guards,
To use the fine art of surprise,
They accosted the men and with two score and ten,
Drove them out of the bay of Belsize.

Back home, the cat was unaware,
As he closed his weary eyes,
Of the secrets betrayed by the cake he had made,
And how it had stopped their demise.

Later that day, a sentry arrived,
To summon him by regal decree,
A crowd was assembled, the pussycat trembled,
Just what was his fate to be?

The queen appeared and told the crowd,
The fantastical tale of how,
With the whimsical cake he'd unwittingly baked,
The village was safe… for now.

Patacake Cat was awarded a medal,
To loud resounding cheers,
She offered to keep him in luxury steeped,
For the rest of his livelong years.

Patacake graciously thanked the Queen,
But declined and farewell bade,
To return to his days in the flour dust haze,
Of the bakery where his bed was made.

Truth was, the cat had realised that,
He quite liked his life with Gus.
No amount of fame or a Queen's acclaim,
Could keep him from being his puss.

And though he was pleased that the village was saved,
By his wonderful, magical cake,
Some measure your worth and value by how,
Much use of you they can make.

The cat learned that to be a friend,
Means to give as well as to take,
And that, dear friends, truly was,
The icing upon the cake.

Author's Note

For Gracie-Rose, Caleb, Zachary, Jessica, Morgan, Harley and Erin.

Thank you to E. Rachael Hardcastle for believing in the magic of cats and cake.

Thank you to the wonderful Sarah Painting for bringing my story to life.

And thank you to Otis, Enzo and Phoebe, who inspired this tale and will never know.

Lightning Source UK Ltd.
Milton Keynes UK
UKHW051015260821
389501UK00006B/96

9 781999 968885